TelTel Series

The Dance

Party

Book One

TelTel Series

The Dance

Party

Book One

K.B. Onyango

Published by Sahel Publishing Association,
a subsidiary of Sahel Books Inc.
P.O. Box 18007—00100
Nairobi, Kenya
Tel: +011-254-715-596-106
For questions and orders log on to:
www.sahelpublishing.net

A Sahel Book
Nairobi. New Delhi. London. Nashville.
Editor: Sam Okello
Interior design and cover by Hellen Wahonya Okello
Images: Courtesy google.com
Printed in USA

This book is dedicated to my children Junior, Michelle and Hadassah

Acknowledgement

The *Dance Party* is proof of what teamwork can achieve in a short time. Following in the footstep of my grandfather, who was a great storyteller, I had the manuscript written, but publishing it took the combined effort of a great team.

I am heavily indebted to my colleagues Andrew, Jane, Emily, Elizabeth, Mary, Jared Elvine, Verah and Winfridah, who kept encouraging me to go on and have the book published.

I may not have sufficient words of praise for my friend George Ogembo, who took my project as his own and gave me support and encouragement. It is a standing ovation to my publisher, Sahel Publishing Association, which worked with incredible speed and diligence to have the book published in the shortest time possible.

Last but not least, my family was there for me all the time as I weaved the stories together. Without their support, understanding and positive attitude, it would have taken much longer to have this book published.

Table of Contents

One

THE BIG QUACK

In many rural villages in Africa, teachers are among the most senior officers of the government. Of course there a few other government employees, but they are just a drop in the sea. If anything, they live faraway in the big towns and only come on special occasions.

This leaves the teachers as the main drivers of the village economy.

This has made teachers to be respected in the rural set ups. They teach the children and help them grow up to be good members of our society.

Next to the teachers are the artisans or *fundis*, as they are popularly known. They include anybody, ranging from a labourer to a technician. Most of them are semi-skilled and therefore are needed to fix a few problems here and there. The services they provide are not the problem; the problem is the fact that they can fix just about anything.

Take the example of this one *fundi* who went to look for employment in the city. He worked at a construction site in the city for one month and when he came back, he started bragging that he was able to fix any problem in the village. He would plaster a house, repair a radio and even treat sick cows in the village. He became a mister know it all.

One time a villager's radio broke down. It was brought to the *fundi* for repair. He demanded that the radio owner buy a new carburetor for the radio to work.

In another case a villager injured his toe while weeding in the garden and the *fundi* injected him right by the wound. Through a miracle, some of the problems he attempted to fix actually got fixed. Like in the case of the radio, the owner did not know where to buy a carburetor but gave him money anyway. The following day the radio worked!

After six months of work in the village, the *fundi's* fame grew in leaps and bounds. People would consult him on all matters. It was not uncommon to hear somebody ask him when he would fix the radio even as he was busy plastering a house.

The risk this *fundi* posed was very high, but the villagers were always willing to take it. People came from far and wide to consult him. Maybe because of ignorance or fear, the fundi became the man of the moment. The village was very far from all modern facilities and this is why villagers looked up to the people who come up with a ready solution to their problems. The *fundi* did that and was rewarded with loyalty.

Two

AMIN THE TERROR

A man called Bandeko lived in a far village. He was popularly known as Goro Bandeko, which happened not to be his real name. He lived alone after his wife died and was fond of keeping dogs. He was an expert hunter and would return home with game meat each time he went hunting. His dogs were trained to chase and catch animals by the throat. Once the catch was lying still, they barked to call Bandeko. If anybody dared touch their catch, they sank their ferocious teeth into the victim.

Of all Bandeko's dogs, one called Amin was outstanding. Relatively bigger and stronger, compared to the rest, Amin rarely caught 'small' animals like the hare. It always went for the gazelles, antelopes and the like. When an antelope was spotted, Amin would outrun the pack of dogs and wrestle the animal to the ground. The only exception was when there was a fence because while a typical antelope jumped over the fence for dear life Amin could not jump.

Once the catch was wrestled down, none would dare move near it except Bandeko. Any dog coming near the dead animal would get a bite of its life; and the same applied to other hunters. So Amin was loved and hated in equal measure. Loved because Amin would ensure enough game meat to share and hated because it was a champion hunting dog, ensuring Bandeko was the one to share out meat.

After a while Amin developed strange behavior. It never went hunting; it instead remained at home, guarding Bandeko's homestead. Amin ensured nobody visited the home or parked a car within the home when Bandeko was away.

As if he had changed roles or just retired from hunting, Amin became a home guard. It guarded the home with so much vigour that people nicknamed him Amin the Terror. Nobody, no animal, no chicken was allowed in the home except one of their own. Even birds flying over the home were chased away. This went on for six months, then one morning Amin was found dead next to Bandeko's house.

Three

THE WATER VENDOR

In Situlo village there was a young farmer called Chune. He was so hardworking and so determined to succeed that he tried growing varied crops every time and everywhere he had an opportunity to. After a few years of hard work he had a herd of cattle, sheep and goats.

One day Chune heard there were cows that could produce up to fifty litres of milk per day. He wanted to see these wonderful cows because the ones he had could hardly produce two liters each per day.

Out of his savings, he made a journey to the place he was told such cows were. To Chune's amazement, he saw the milkman arrive with an empty pail to milk, but later, after milking, the pail was full with milk. Chune made a decision to have even one such cow instead of having ten cows, which hardly brought in seven litres per day.

After the fact-finding mission and a strong resolve, Chune sold all his cows, leaving only two bulls for ploughing. He used the money to buy the wonder cows and the very first week all roads led to Chune's home for milk.

In no time word reached a local mission hospital about the milk and the management asked Chune to be supplying them milk. Beaming, Chune added more cows and all his efforts were finally channeled in the production of milk.

Demand for Chune's milk, at the mission hospital, increased by the day. Soon they wanted sixty liters of milk every morning. Caught off guard, he thought of a brilliant idea. He would avail fifty five liters of milk and top up with water to make it sixty liters. He was so smart that it was difficult to catch him because he would put the five liters of water in the pail first and then add milk to it!

One day Chune went to pick his pay from the mission hospital. After he got the money, he put all of it in his breast pocket and rode his bicycle back home. That day was hot and dusty. On reaching the stream, just before his home, he thought of washing his face in the cool stream.

As he bent, all the money dropped in the stream and it was washed away.

From that day on, Chune learnt the importance of honesty and need to use accurate measures. He told those who would listen to him how things were promising when he was honest and how things had changed the moment he started adding water to his milk. "I was vending water and that is why water took its share of the money after it had enough of my trickery," he said.

Four

SPWAP, THE BROTHER'S ENEMY

In Wagure village, there is the interesting story of a man called Obila. He had eight daughters and two sons. In those days, having a daughter meant riches because once she got married the family would receive many cows as dowry. With eight daughters, Obila would one day be the proud owner of more than one hundred heads of cattle. This was because more than ten cows would be paid for each of his daughters.

His two sons, Gango and Spwap, would be rich too because they were heirs to their father's wealth.

Ordinarily, the elder brother was favoured in many ways. He was polite and nice to all people. He was kind, unlike his younger brother, who was rude. Spwap, the younger of the brothers, schemed to acquire more of the wealth than his elder brother. So when his sisters got married and cows were brought in as dowry, he grew weary of the presence of his brother, Gango.

One day Spwap thought of a plan; a plan not just to inherit more cows than his elder brother, but to inherit all of his father's wealth.

As tradition required, Gango had to be blessed and given a place to build his home. His younger brother, Spwap, would remain in the home to take care of their aging parents. This was done and wealth appropriately distributed.

After the death of their parents, Spwap also built his own home in contravention of culture. He later visited a witchdoctor, who gave him charm to pour at Gango's gate. This charm would kill Gango's family one by one. Ultimately Spwap would remain with everything.

Spwap did what the witchdoctor had told him and after a few days Gango's wife fell ill and died. This was followed by Gango's eldest son. He died too.

Luckily, Gango's youngest son, Mito, stayed with his maternal uncle far away. This charm never affected him. He was the only surviving member of Gango's family.

After the death of Gango's family, Spwap fell ill. He ran back to the witchdoctor, who told him his family was next. This caused a quarrel between Spwap and the witchdoctor. Spwap had all along thought his family would be safe.

Unknown to him, a small portion of the charm had remained in the jar and he had accidentally poured a few drops at his own gate. The few drops were potent enough to kill all of them because his whole family was at home.

That way Gango's lastborn son, Mito, was the sole survivor and heir to his grandfather's entire wealth.

Five

TALES OF THE GRAVEYARD

To the south of Mutune village there is a place called graveyard. It is a graveyard because young warriors from that village, who died at war, are buried there. That graveyard is in front of the wall-fenced village, apparently to guard the village against intruders. Years after the somber burials, villagers moved more than a kilometer away from the place, so it remained an exclusive graveyard zone, where the spirits of the dead warriors lived.

There were reports that voices could be heard at the graveyard and the smell of aromatic food would emanate from there. Parties too were held in that place, where there were no homes! People were discouraged from passing near the graveyard early in the morning and late in the evening. Unconfirmed reports had it that the spirits knew all the people in the village and when a strange face passed by they were heard asking who the stranger was.

One day a visitor came from far away and asked for accommodation in a village neighbouring the graveyard. He liked the place and later he asked if he could stay in the village. He was given the open land near the graveyard. He built a house there. That very night, spirits from the graveyard came around and demanded to know who had allowed the man to build in their path.

This coming night, they warned, they would kill everybody in the house if the man did not go away. This man left the place before dawn!

It was reported also that a group of boys were running to joining a dance party. They heard voices around the graveyard. They thought it was their colleagues who were going ahead of them. They shouted, "Hey, wait for us we go together!"

As they were running past the graves, they saw nobody but heard laughter from behind them. That was the last time anybody ever walked around that place at night.

There were no reports of anybody ever being attacked by the spirits. The sweet smell from the graveyard became less and less with time.

Less of the stories were told about the place as time lapsed.

There were allegations that the gardens around the place were stolen from, but that must have been petty thieves stealing and claiming the spirits had stolen.

Today it remains tales told by grandparents and parents. Since they tell the story in the same style and manner, who knows whether the spirits really existed or not?

Six

KINDAKI THE NIGHT RUNNER

A village is not complete without a few misfits. Misfits range from thieves to night runners to drunkards to the laziest of the lazy.

Otomo village was no exception because it had its own share of misfits. One of them was Kindaki the night runner.

At night villagers locked their doors in fear of this night runner. Many nights his footsteps could be heard outside and everyone would freeze under their blankets. He used a stick to disturb the night, grinding it against the roof as he walked from house to house.

One day boys in the village had a meeting. They discussed the matter and concluded, "We are all boys, growing up to be men. If the five of us are afraid of one night runner then how will we defend our families? If we do not stop him our village has no warriors. He must be stopped and it must be done today!"

But the plan could not be put to work because that very night he came and threw sand on the boys. None of the boys was brave enough to as much as turn in his bed, let alone get out. Not even a single boy had strength to go for a short call. That night Kindaki went on a rampage, kicking people's doors, throwing sand and all sorts of funny things at the roofs.

This continued for two years!

As the boys grew older and stronger and went to secondary school, one of them shared his predicament with schoolmates. When he came back for the holidays, he brought a permanent solution to the problem. According to his friend, the night runner had to be from the area, so they needed to start a loud discussion near the suspect's home, how they would catch him or her. When they did that, the night runner never came that night, so they became convinced it had to be Kindaki.

The following night the night runner threw live rats at the boys. That scared them stiff, but they were not ready to cede any ground. They walked out of the room and announced aloud that the night runner will curse the day he returns to the boys' home.

The next time he came, the night runner threw sand at the boys and took off. They gave chase, but they never caught him.

School opened and all the boys went back to consult with their friends. Their friends gave different ideas about how to deal with the menace.

December holidays came and the boys compared notes. It was resolved that they seal all openings in the fence, allowing passage at the main and side gates only. Their father was so happy that the boys were weeding the compound and repairing the fence without waiting for his instructions. This was done to seal possible escape routes from the compound.

On the appointed day, one of the boys came late, as planned. The rest had set a rope knee-high at the side gate, purposefully to trap the cunning night runner.

When John returned through the main gate and shouted "I've seen him!" they all rushed out and gave chase. The night runner tripped while trying to escape through the side gate and fell with a thud. When the boys reached him, Kindaki pleaded for his life and that was the end of his night running!

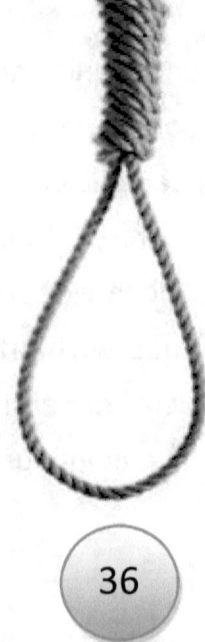

Seven

THE DANCE PARTY

A long long time ago parties, especially those where people danced, were a rare occurrence in the villages. Only towards the end of the year could one see a few parties organized.

Most such parties were held at night and thus the following day's activities were sometimes disrupted. Those who lived in towns might have had the advantage of enjoying shows that had a mix of local and foreign bands playing to entertain them, but not the humble villagers.

In the village the only time such shows were put on display was when someone died.

After burial, music would play for about two to three hours every night till the following weekend. The problem with such parties was that people would not die that frequently, so it took long for villagers to have a dance.

Whenever an elderly person died there was a chance for prolonged dancing because his or her extended relatives would be coming to mourn. The more daughters one had the merrier, because in-laws would try to outdo one another in entertaining the villagers.

One day an old lady passed on in the village. She had two sons and six daughters, who were all married. This meant there would be six dancing sessions when each son-in-law came to mourn his loving mother-in-law.

People in the village could not wait to see for themselves. Those were the days when discos were taking root in the region. Most villagers had only heard of discos, but not seen one. They were used to simple turntables, which could not be heard from one hundred meters away. The gossip was whether one of the sons-in-law would bring a disco to the village.

As it turned out, none of the sons-in-law brought a disco, but the machines each brought were very good. People enjoyed the dance and, to their amazement, there were many new songs they had not heard before. Many villagers wished the old lady had died towards the end of the year. Oh the music was really good!

One of the dancing sessions did not go very well. There was a misunderstanding that brought the party to a premature end. One of the sons-in-law had brought a good machine, with the latest hits, but he also brought nice-looking ladies who danced well.

That was a mistake!

Tradition in the village had it that visitors danced with local girls and local boys danced with visiting ladies. But one of the visiting ladies would not dance with the locals!

Trouble started when one of the local boys asked if she could dance with him, but she responded in a language that appeared foreign. That was when everybody noticed that even her dressing was different.

Her hair was plaited and she had a ribbon. Why she could not speak in the local language was another big puzzle. The master of ceremony declared she must dance, but she looked blankly at everybody.

At that point, the visiting boys explained that she did not understand the local language and should be exempted. The local boys would hear none of it and insisted on dancing with her.

In the heat of the mix up, somebody threw a stone at the pressure lamp and a ball of fire erupted. Everyone scampered for safety, leaving the poor girl too scared to move. She cried in the local language, suddenly forgetting she had been a foreign girl.

She was lucky she was not hurt, but her story did rounds in the village and back at her home, especially how she had pretended not to understand only to wail in the very language she could not understand moments before!

Eight

THE STRANGE VISITOR

At the beginning of the year a strange visitor came to Monuch village. Nobody in the village knew him or where he had come from. Nobody knew his relatives, but he remained perched on top of a tall tree as if all was well.

He looked like a monkey but his colour was darker, his face whiter and a little bigger—and he had a white line with long hair at the back. The noise he made was different from all the monkeys that had been encountered around.

This was a highly superstitious village that believed in many odd things. People started stories about this strange visitor. Later, with the passing of time, word went round and people from neighbouring villages gathered to see this new visitor. In no time people from villages yonder crossed the waist-deep river to see the strange visitor.

One woman thought it was her dead relative who had come back in the form of a monkey. She pleaded with the monkey to allow her more time to complete the assignment she was given. One man thought it was Jesus Christ who had come in form of a monkey. He declared it was the end of the world!

People cooked up different theories and argued loudly about the visitor. But there were those who simply brought bananas and other fruits that the monkey gladly took and ate.

Then there were those who brought bread and other goodies, much to his excitement of the monkey. For a better part of the morning, there was speculation about the creature, where it came from and why it visited the village.

The party went on well until someone called the press. The reporter was told people woke up only to find a strange animal perched on a tree in the village. He was told everybody had tried to guess what the strange animal was, but people were not too sure—it just looked like a monkey, that's all they knew.

The reporter dashed to the scene where he found a beehive of activity. Some were praying, others too shocked to utter a word, others calling the names of their ancestors, while the home owner was ready to vacate his home following a visit by the strange animal.

Finally the reporter went on air highlighting the morning's events, while showing clips of people responding to news of the visitor. He explained that it was a Columbus monkey!

Nine

PAUL AND HIS CAKES

In a country called Kionge there lived the very modern family of Mr. and Mrs. Ntumbwenye. This family lived in the capital city, Bokoyo. Like the other families in the city, the Ntumbwenye's had a rural home some four hundred kilometers west of the capital. Mr. Ntumbwenye's parents and other relatives lived in the rural home. Towards the end of the year, this family usually travelled to the rural home to reunite with their friends and family members.

The Ntumbwenye family was blessed with a boy called Paul. Paul was the last born child in the family. His elder brother and sister were in college. He was a lively boy, loved by all.

Paul so loved his rural home that at times he would travel with some of his relatives to the home even if it was not the end of the year.

Paul had a unique liking for cakes. He would request his parents to buy for him cakes. At times his mother baked cakes at home for him. Paul loved homemade cakes because he ate a lot of it. If one wanted to make Paul happy, all he had to do was buy a cake for him.

One day Paul wanted to visit his cousins in the rural home. It was not the end of the year, but he really wanted to go to the rural home. No amount of persuasion would make Paul change his mind.

In the end his parents agreed and the date of travel was fixed.

Paul was very excited and eagerly awaited the journey. He remembered the long journey and kept reminding his parents of the towns he would pass before reaching home.

He said: From this place I will pass through Shiumbo, Mtokwi, Utomoni, then Mavele, where Grandmother will be waiting. The four towns were about one hundred kilometers apart, along the long, winding way.

On the day of the journey, Mother packed four pieces of cake for Paul and instructed him to eat the first piece at Shiumbo, and others at

Mtokwi, Utomoni and Mavele. He was told to carry the bigger cake home and share with his cousins. This got him so excited!

Paul sat in the front seat, between the driver and another passenger. Barely ten minutes into the journey, he started asking the driver whether they had reached Shiumbo. He repeated the question three times in twenty minutes, so the driver assured Paul that when they reach Shiumbo he would tell Paul.

All went smoothly thereafter. As the van passed Shiumbo, Paul was not informed. After a long time and about forty kilometers past Shiumbo, Paul asked the driver again whether Shiumbo was still far away. Some of the passengers started scolding the driver, forcing him to turn the vehicle and drive back to Shiumbo.

When the driver reached Shiumbo, he stopped the van and told Paul that it was the place. To everybody's surprise, Paul opened his bag and took a piece of cake and ate it.

The passengers who had not scolded the driver started shouting at the other passengers.

One said it would have been better to ask the boy what the problem was rather than scold the driver. He went on to say, "We have wasted time and now we have to start a fresh. We have done one hundred and twenty kilometers only for the boy to eat his cake!"

The rest of the journey went smoothly after Paul explained where he needed to eat the other pieces!

Ten

BABY GIRL! BABY GIRL!!

The saying goes: *All work and no play makes Jack a dull boy.* I have always wondered whether Jane is the opposite of Jack, meaning: *All play and no work makes Jane a happy girl.*

That was one of my many thoughts as we played in our rural home. It was fun, fun and more fun!

As a young boy I remember rope-jumping while singing a song I could never make sense of and I still wonder whether I ever will. I have asked a few friends from the east and the west but all they seem to agree on is the tune, the pace, the tone and the pauses. What they sang, or remember singing, is totally different!

I also wonder who set rules for these games and how they seemed to be so uniform in application east, west, north and south. Since the games were played everywhere, I have a feeling the games originated from one place and were spread by migrating people like tourist, missionaries or even colonialists.

Of all the games, rope-jumping, with participants in queue joining to sing something, which went like this:

Bubble gum, bubble gum Number Twenty Eight
I went for a walk but no, yes and I stood
and a break...
[pause]
Zero point zero is a round, round all down.
I am a girl this is the factory I must do.
Salute for the king, bend for the queen, shut
your eyes and count fifteen. One, two...

...was the best.

Is there a game you enjoy today? What language was it in and do you remember the words correctly? Do you remember what the rules of the game were?